DARK PLANET COMICS presents

SILVER

by
STEPHAN FRANCK

DARK PLANET COMICS presents

SILVER

By
STEPHAN FRANCK

Volume 1
Finnigan
Sledge
Curse Of The Silver Dragon

DARK PLANET COMICS

www.DarkPlanetComics.com

Published by Dark Planet, Inc. Silver Volume 1 is Copyright © 2014 Stephan Franck. James Finnigan™, Rosalynd "Sledge" Van-Helsing ™, and all other prominently featured characters are trademarks of Stephan Franck. Dark Planet® and the Dark Planet logo are trademarks of Dark Planet, Inc. All rights reserved. No portion of this publication may be reproduced or transmitted, in any form or by any means (except for short excerpts for review purposes) without the express written permission of Dark Planet, Inc. Names, characters, places, and incidents featured in this publication are entirely fictional. Any resemblance to actual persons (living or dead), events or places, without satiric intent, is coincidental.

Printed in Canada

CHAPTER ONE:
FINNIGAN

Written & Illustrated by STEPHAN FRANCK

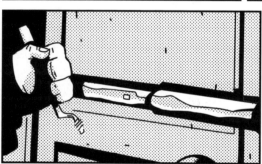

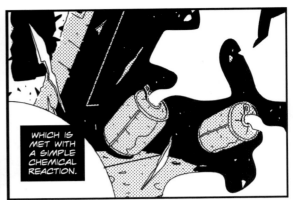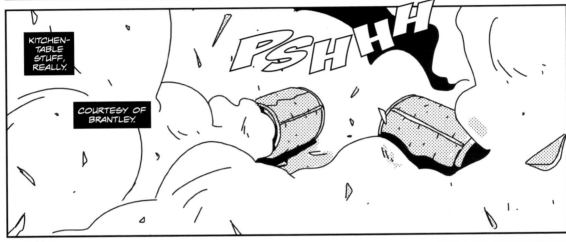

SAY WHAT YOU WILL ABOUT CARNIES...

IT'S MOMENTS LIKE THESE THAT MAKE ME THINK MY TWO YEARS WITH THAT CIRCUS--

--WEREN'T A COMPLETE WASTE OF TIME.

IN FACT, THOSE TWO YEARS JUST BOUGHT ME--

--ANOTHER THIRTY SECONDS OF LIFE!

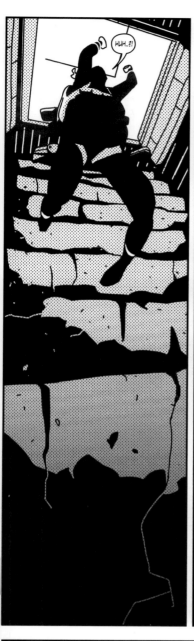

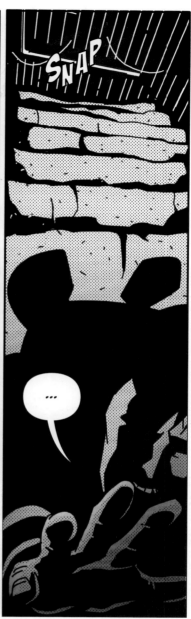

SOMETIMES I LIKE TO REMIND MYSELF OF WHO I AM--

WOW...

JAMES FINNIGAN.

SCOUNDREL. FAKESTER. CON-MAN. THIEF.

THE KIND OF GUY WHO DOESN'T SPOOK EASILY.

WELL--

GO AHEAD.

COUNT ME SPOOKED.

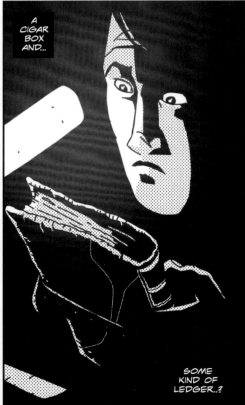

CHAPTER TWO:
SLEDGE

Written & Illustrated
by
STEPHAN FRANCK

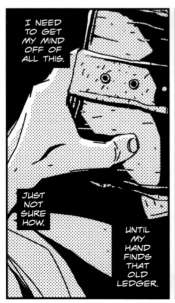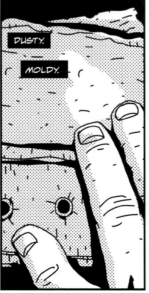

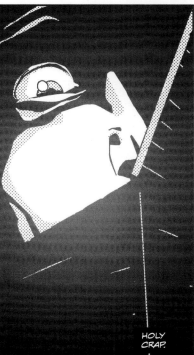

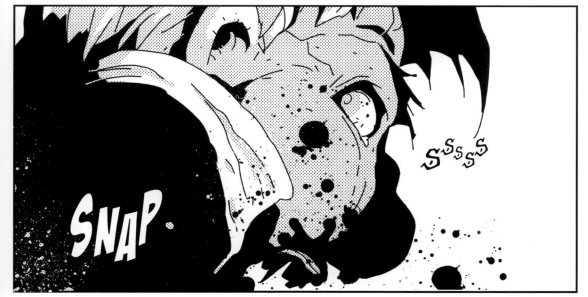

CHAPTER THREE:
CURSE OF THE SILVER DRAGON

*Written & Illustrated
by
STEPHAN FRANCK*

BEHIND THE PAGES

SILVER started its life in movie script form. In that format, visual cues are sparse, only written in if absolutely necessary. The focus is on the character's voices and the momentum of the story. Essentially, the scriptwriter is leaving the directing to the director. So here, most of the "directing" happened as I laid out the pages. For me, storytelling is an iterative process, and many of the choices get revisited and refined as pages get bumped up to the next stage.

Since the script gave no indication of page-count in comic format, the first decisions had to do with pacing. My goal was to decompress the storytelling enough to give the moments depth and texture, creating a nice immersive experience for the reader who enters the world of Silver, while keeping the story moving at a good clip. As it turned out, 1 page of script translated on average into 3 pages of comic. Movie scripts are also usually structured in 10-page increments, where some sort of turn happen every 10 pages. Those offered natural breaks for each chapter. The 120-page script divided nicely into a 12-issue miniseries (each issue being 29 pages).

My approach to laying out comic book pages borrows a lot from my experience with film language. When I storyboard, I am always mindful of what kind of lens I am presenting the scene through. How much background do I see? How is that lens connecting with the characters? I also try to have my shots cut as smoothly as possible as to not disrupt the storytelling. No awkward jump cuts or weird changes of screen direction (unless it's on purpose), horizon lines under control, etc... Here, I try to have my panels function along the same visual principles. Some of it already works in the layouts, some of it, I improve along the way.

Once the inks are final, I revisit the page to polish dialog and narration. Sometimes, the extra text comes in to bridge a visual gap in the action that I didn't want to expand into more panels. Sometimes, the extra narration is also useful to control the timing of the reader's experience as well as adding a

It's interesting to see that the bit about "there are two kinds of objects in this world..." originally wasn't in the script. It presented itself when I was doing the layouts, first just for texture. It eventually became a key motif for Finn.

Page 20 has two significant changes from layouts to finals. The first one is panel A. In the finals, the camera is more "on axis" looking straight at the kid. That makes for a better cut between panel A and B, because B is also seen from the side. A being more frontal avoids visual repetition. The final version also offers a clearer point of view—Finn's—and involves us more directly in the moment.

The other change from roughs to finals happens on the last panel of page 20. First, the perspective was off. To see the cops' upper bodies and still being able to see the kid would have been difficult. Also, I felt that I had already seen enough of the cops' backs. Lastly, the rough version really made the shot about the cops, and their discovery of the scene, while I felt that the moment should be about the kid bracing himself for their arrival. For all those reasons, I changed the panel in the finals, making it completely about the kid. All lines are converging towards him, and some giant nameless boots are charging in.

By contrast, page 21 hasn't changed at all. The final version is just about drawing the stuff in and solidifying the perspective, and adding textural details. The only change: the kid is more centered, standing still as they swarm around him. I also used the intersection of the checkered floor tiles to frame him with maximum contrast: white against black and black against white.

Since the first issue came out, I've been asked a lot of questions about doing a page with heavy blacks, and on how to keep it all legible.

The first challenge is to get the individual panels to read. The thinking is simple. Visual objects are defined by only a few key "inflection points" such as angles, changes of direction, or signature shapes. For instance, a cube is defined by its corners. A house is defined by the area where the roof shape and the walls intersect, etc... So it's okay to obscure as much of the rest of the shape as you want, as long as the inflection points are left visible.

On the overall page, you want to make sure that the black areas within one panel don't look like the continuation of other black shapes in an adjacent panel. If they did, the eye would read these areas as continuous shapes across panels, which would destroy the storytelling. The black areas across the page have to be broken up as to not coalesce into one giant meta shape that flows across panels, and takes over the page.

n this next page, the staging didn't change much between layouts and finals. Panels A to D stay very close to the roughs. The biggest change is on Panel E. In the layout, the vampire crawling down the wall had a generic undead kind of feel. On the final page, I wanted a more specific Hammer Film-type eerie-vampire-babe-in-a-night-gown kind of thing. I also felt that the original panel had a focus problem, as both characters were given equal importance. To focus on the vampire, I edged Finn out of the shot, and recreated the feel of a camera moving past Finn to find the vampire. That's also why I rendered Finn with less details—to give the sensation that he was out of focus, without using any actual blur filter on the drawing, as that wouldn't fit the style of the book.

Page 21, by contrast, has changed a lot. The original reason for the change was to try to avoid visual repetition. I felt that, by that point, we had already seen enough of Sledge in a stalking stance with Finn in tow. I also thought that the money in this case was the vampire's big reveal. So I gave him the full page, playing the shot as Finn's point of view.

On a process level, this is also a good example of my work-flow. Layouts in Photoshop, final inks in Manga Studio, and then back to Photoshop if fancy brushes are requested for a spattering effect.

Interestingly, taking Sledge out of page 21 meant that I had to change the first Panel of page 22. In the rough she used to be right in front of Finn. I thought it would be nice to have her step out of the shadows behind him instead, as if Finn had foolishly passed her and didn't see her, which makes her quite the lurking Ninja. Also notice a different acting choice on Finn.

12A always was a fun panel, but the composition was a little claustrophobic in the rough. In the finals, I opened it up.

There were also perspective problems in the layout: it was a low angle on the cop and kid, yet, a shoulder-level view of Finn. That kind of inconsistency would have been hard to resolve in the finals, so I had to fix the perspective.

Right before I was to draw the finals on that page, I took a fortuitous trip to NYC. I shot tons of reference pictures, including of the Manhattan Library, which I thought would be a funner location than some generic federal building. So I got the shot I wanted, used it to draw the building, and rejiggled my characters to place them in a more credible perspective, while keeping the idea of the composition.

On page 13, the first three panels were starting to feel a little repetitious with the car, so I tried to vary the angles as much as possible to create three very different images. Also, I thought having the wheel in the foreground in 13C would help focus the attention on Finn, getting us "past the car business".

13D hasn't changed at all, but is one of those panels that really comes alive when the mood comes in. Here too, I blacked out the guys in the foreground to help said mood and composition.

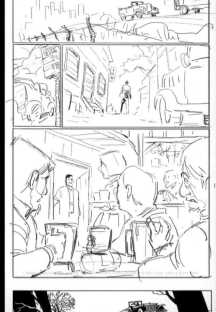

Finally, the panel that probably changed the most is the one below. Let's be honest, it started out a complete mess—crowded, confusing, with an inexpressive and uninteresting angle on the Finn being shot at. First I got rid of the "present-time characters" who are having that mental image. Then, I decided I really wanted to have fun with this panel, and to do a mini Kirby homage—do a little crouched power stance, character looking straight at us... etc... In those cases, for obvious reasons, I always make it a point not to actually look at any actual Kirby drawing. So it just remains a vague impressionistic homage. But at least, I have fun with it.

Somewhere in there, I played with the idea of having the bullets coming at us, then I remembered that the shot was not about bullets, but about seeing the pocket get torn out—duh...

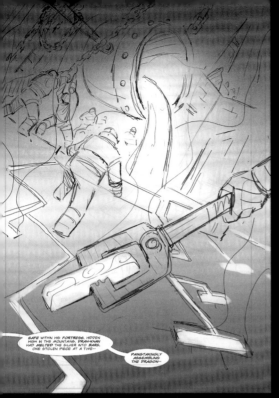

The third issue presented a fun challenge as Finnigan shares the epic backstory behind the curse of the Silver Dragon. I wanted those moments to feel like windows suddenly opening on a different time. A time when ancient gods walked the Earth, and stole silver from mortals to build shining pyramids... anyway, you get the picture... So I decided to go with a run of splash pages.

I was particularly looking forward to the casting of the bars, as that scene would also perfectly lend itself to some kind of a Kirby-esque moment. I can't recall any single piece of comic art that made my head spin like Kirby's Celestials backstory pages in the Eternals. Although I wouldn't even try to create something of that magnitude, I definitely tried to connect with the feeling of it. Here again, I made it a point not to look up any specific reference. Had I done that, I would have ended up just trying to copy it. So instead, I find it more fun to just let my mind access the memory of how those pages made me feel when I was 10 years old, and just try to connect with that impression and use it to do my page.

In this particular case, there is almost no difference between the layout and the final. The only departure is the super heavy use of black on that page. I googled images of foundries to investigate the lighting situation, and those images are so high contrast, that it's almost all black.

For the next page--Drah-Khan, alone, facing the pyramid--I wanted to contrast the bronze age savagery of the previous pages with something almost rarefied and new age-y. So for this one, I was thinking something Mebius-y. Again, not any piece of artwork in particular, just a general impression of what I remember of his crystal period. This is another page that came out very naturally in the roughs, and which had very little change in its final version--except that I spent a couple of hours just drawing that dragon...

y contrast, some of the other pages show a lot of change from roughs to finals, especially page 4, 5 and 6. I was originally trying to keep one foot in the story's present tense, weaving images of Finn and his gang into the pages. Although conceptually interesting, the end result proved too messy, and lacking impact. I ended up taking a chainsaw to those pages, and cutting out Finn & gang entirely. I still miss some of those drawings, but as they say, you have to be able to kill your own babies.

On page 4, having the unobstructed full page to retell the original Bram Stoker act 1 gave it space to breathe. Although the same beats are represented in the finals, there are some notable improvement. I wanted to be more specific about the Victorian feel by showing some London landmarks in the first tableau (although I kept the skyline out of the black ink, doing it with just the zip-a-tones instead, to give depth and evoke a foggy atmosphere) The idea of the dress becoming the stormy skies is meant to evoke 19th century romanticism. I also felt that the last tableau (Dracula silhouetted on the deck of the Demeter) was a missed opportunity to bring scale to the page. That's why I replaced it with the full shot of the ship on the ocean, which also reinforces the romantic imagery.

Page 5 was also streamlined a great deal. Getting rid of Finn and co, and even reducing the Harker poses from 3 to 2 also gave the page clarity and impact, and an opportunity to be more descriptive with the location. The lesson for me is to not try to hit too many beats visually, and give the art's illustrative quality a chance to breathe.

Same deal on page 6. Got rid of the crew. The Bronze age scene also had a few changes. First, I removed Drah-Khan's helmeted head from the shot, and gave more prominence to the gloved hand. I found that in these pages, the more elusive and mysterious I kept him, the better. Also note that I changed the foreground victim from a man to a woman. Back when I worked at Disney, we had a visit from Geena Davis who was doing a tour of the studios to bring to people's attention the fact that female characters were under-represented in stories, not only in lead or supporting role, but in the general population of our fictional universes. She was absolutely right. Out of habit, you usually just put in a dude. So unless it specifically has to be a male, I put in a female character. Plus as far as the impact of the scene, I felt that a young female was more compelling

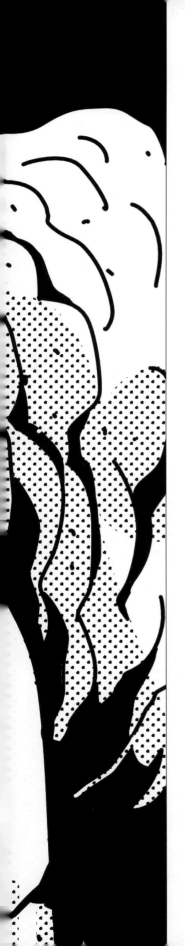

SILVER
GALLERY

Featuring

Rodolphe Guenoden (Rodguen)

Takeshi Miyazawa

Marcello Vignali

Juliaon Roels

Stephan Franck

Stephan Franck -- "Silver"

Rodolphe Guenoden (Rodguen) -- "Sledge At Work"

Takeshi Miyazawa -- "Finnigan & Sledge"

Stephan Franck - Silver #3 cover - inks

Marcello Vignali - "Sledge"

Juliaon Roels -- "Myrick"

ACKNOWLEDGEMENTS

There is a long list of people whose help and inspiration, direct or indirect, somehow went into the creation of this book. The list includes loved ones as well as people I only met through the world of story, and it goes something like this:

To Bram Stoker, respectfully submitted.

To Jack Kirby, Will Eisner, Jim Steranko, for making the world magic.

To Fritz Lang, Todd Browning, Chaplin, Kazan, and all the A, B, and Z masters of black and white who kept the 10 year-old me glued to his TV watching " Le Cinema De Minuit" way past his bedtime every Friday night—I had school on Saturday mornings, you fools!

Thank you to all the old friends who supported me through this. I love you, and you know who you are.

Thank you to all the new friends who discovered SILVER at conventions or online in 2013. Your enthusiasm solidified my belief that this was an adventure worth pursuing, and your relentless championing of SILVER on social media helped make all this possible.

Thank you Sean Eckols and Alan Bodner for helping me with the color of the comics covers and art prints. Your magic has been stopping traffic at conventions.

To all the backers who funded the SILVER Volume 1 Kickstarter campaign, you are absolutely amazing, and you helped make this edition possible in a tremendous way.

To my brother Emmanuel, partner in crime for life, and Francine my wonderful mom, who freaked out when she saw me read Kirby's ETERNALS at age 8, but chose to say nothing and let me do it anyway.

To my Dad, for looking like a cross between Humphrey Bogart and Martin Landau and knowing how it all works.

And finally, but most importantly, to Christina, Theo, Adele and Madeleine. I love you and you mean everything to me, but you already know that.

Los Angeles, February 2014